T0195883

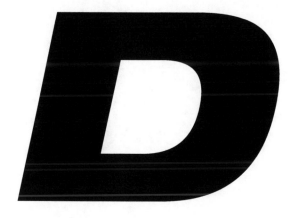

EUGENE O. BAILEY

authorHOUSE®

AuthorHouse™
1663 Liberty Drive
Bloomington, IN 47403
www.authorhouse.com
Phone: 833-262-8899

This is a work of fiction. All of the characters, names, incidents, organizations, and dialogue in this novel are either the products of the author's imagination or are used fictitiously.

Published by AuthorHouse 10/14/2021

ISBN: 978-1-6655-4008-7 (sc)
ISBN: 978-1-6655-4007-0 (hc)
ISBN: 978-1-6655-4014-8 (e)

Library of Congress Control Number: 2021920182

Print information available on the last page.

Any people depicted in stock imagery provided by Getty Images are models, and such images are being used for illustrative purposes only. Certain stock imagery © Getty Images.

This book is printed on acid-free paper.

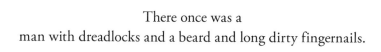

There once was a
man with dreadlocks and a beard and long dirty fingernails.

He was born with
Polydactili and Hypospaidious.

He had just got out of jail for smoking weed.

His mom worked very hard and was a single mother with two boys.

He had a bully and his name was Calvin.

Calvin had dreads and a beard and was a ninja.

Calvin would take his money.

Calvin would beat D up.

Calvin would take D's condoms.

D was a nice guy so he did not want to fight with Calvin.

D groomed himself and was well kempt.

Calvin was jealous of D for the pettiest of reasons.

One day D met a woman.

D's woman was a supersize big booty woman. SSBBW.

Calvin had a woman but his woman was immature.

Calvin slumped in to an abusive relation.

Calvin was obsessed with his woman.

One day, Calvin picked up a gun and shot at the floor of his girl.

D's relationship was lovely and romantic.

D bought his girl nice things.

Her name was Radell but everybody called her R.

D and R had a baby and it had Polydactyli and Hypospaidious.

After D and R had their son Calvin was removed from reality.

Calvin's girl had an abortion and a tuboligation.

D kept his job and relaxed with a nice blunt after work.

Calvin was a hothead.

Calvin purchased guns.

R started giving D money.

This infuriated Calvin.

This had Calvin sizzling.

R started taking D traveling.

They left Highpoint North Carolina and visited Indonesia.

D and R made love in the jungle.

They woke up the next morning to a blunt on the balcony of their hotel.

R swore to protect D.

Nine months later they had a baby girl.

Calvin started to shout.

Calvin's girl left him for D.

Calvin went to prison for fighting and guns.

D's new girl's name was Maria.

When Calvin got out, Calvin pulled a knife on D.

D told Calvin "to get the hell on"!

D was determined to not lose his job.

Crazy Calvin came back around.

One night R asked Calvin, "Do you want to go to Heaven"?

Calvin started doing cocaine.

Calvin thought cocaine was his way in to heaven.

Calvin overdosed.

D's new girl was Maria but everybody called her M.

M, R, and D had threesomes.

D knew right from wrong.

Calvin tore up books.

Calvin tried to play the victim in all this.

White girls loved D.

Calvin groped and molested girls intentionally.

M took D to California.

Nine months later M and D adopted a fifteen year old daughter.

The daughter's name was Kelly but everybody called her K.

Calvin became more narcissistic, self-centered, and withdrawn.

Calvin started using crystal meth and had hallucinations.

Calvin contemplated suicide.

He then shaved all his hair off.

Calvin tattooed horns on his face and became
a minister of an impecunious church.

Calvin believed in 116:3, 4 out of the bible.

D loved smoking weed with R because R had proven to be the infatuation of his soul.

One day, D decided to give Calvin a piece offering.

The piece offering was an African-American woman.

This was D's way of saying no harm, no foul.

D is the king of his better well thought out choices, and deciding his future.

Calvin moved to Mexico where he never returned.

The End

C the Black Sea Monster

C the black sea monster loved girls. Especially teenage
girls. About twenty two or twenty-three years of
age. The black sea monster had black fur.

One day, he arose from the sea and began to taste their clitorises. Every girl would lay down by the Atlantic and pacific sea board.

A sixty-three year old woman named Ursa was very jealous
of C the monster and wanted to stop his pleasure. Ursa
was menopausal. In many ways she was like the matriarch
CORETTA SCOTT KING in the EBONY magazine.

There was a man named LEE HARVEY OSWALD buried
in North Carolina near the Tennessee boarder.

Four kids loved E dolls except for the second child
named Dexter and his Caucasian tenderoni.

The Caucasian tenderoni became the chief justice
of the supreme court in Washington D.C.

Liken, to, Amy Comey Barett.

Mrs. ROE had an abortion. Mrs. Wade was pure
and had never been tainted herself.

Then Mrs. ACB gave out birth control pills to all the E doll lovers!

10-13, all the skies where blue, the weather warm with sunshine.

The moon was out like Easter Monday sunrise services. Never would there ever be no pain, suffering, sorrow, or storms.

In memory of NCDL number
The year took place in 2027 A.D.
0000004594599.

-Jordan A. Jefferson

Printed in the United States
by Baker & Taylor Publisher Services